DO NOT DISTURB THE DRAGONS

Michelle Robinson

Sh

D1078525

BLOOMSBURY
CHILDREN'S BOOKS

LONDON OXFORD NEW YORK NEW DELHI SYDNEY

BLOOMSBURY CHILDREN'S BOOKS
Bloomsbury Publishing Plc
50 Bedford Square, London WC1B 3DP, UK

BLOOMSBURY, BLOOMSBURY CHILDREN'S BOOKS
and the Diana logo are trademarks of Bloomsbury Publishing Plc

First published in Great Britain in 2020 by Bloomsbury Publishing Plc

A catalogue record for this book is available from the British Library

ISBN: PB: 978-1-4088-9488-0; eBook: 978-1-4088-9487-3

2 4 6 8 10 9 7 5 3 1

Printed and bound in Great Britain by CPI Group (UK) Ltd,
Croydon CR0 4YY

To find out more about our authors and books visit www.bloomsbury.com
and sign up for our newsletters

For Grace Weatherburn, real-life Wonder
– Miche

To Neve and Alex, always
– SD

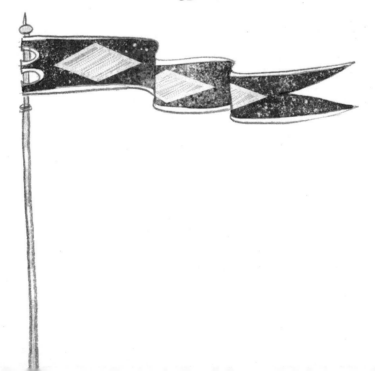

CONTENTS

DO NOT DISTURB THE DRAGONS

It was the first and most important rule in Wondermere:

DO NOT disturb the dragons.

The other nine hundred and forty-six rules were there to make sure the *first* rule was never broken. Rules like:

DO NOT distract the knights
who *guard* the dragons,

DO NOT dilly-dally beneath the
castle turrets

and DEFINITELY DO NOT
attempt to climb them. Seriously.
Don't even think about it –
especially you, Princess Grace.

No kidding. That one time was enough.

To be fair, Grace was only two years old
when she climbed up into the dragon's nest.
Too young to know any better. And she
wasn't a princess at the time. In fact she'd
never even been to the castle before.

She'd arrived on the orphan cart. The

guard knights were so busy
cooing at the other babies
they'd momentarily forgotten
all about the dragons. They
didn't notice Grace slipping
out of the cart, toddling
across the courtyard and
gazing up at the tallest
turret.

The turrets of
Wondermere Castle were
much like those of any
other – except for the
dragons' nests right at
the top. They made the
perfect nesting site.
They were the
highest point for

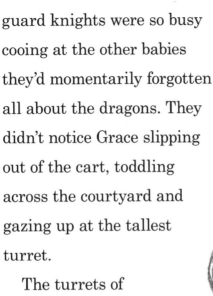

miles, giving the dragons a clear view over their hunting grounds.

The dragons hunted for *sparkle* – and they didn't have to go far to find it.

The surrounding forests were coated in pixie dust. The hills wore soft blankets of sparkling spangle moss. Gold, diamonds and rubies glittered in every rock, stone and pebble from the south coast to the north. Even on a dull day, Wondermere put on the glitz – and the dragons' nests gave the biggest *bling* of all.

Grace had never seen anything so *sparkly*.

A particularly chunky diamond seemed to wink at her. The nest looked so pretty and cosy... Much more appealing than the back of a crowded cart.

The guard knights were distracted.

Grace dilly-dallied.

But not for long. She started to climb the turret.

Grace wrapped her pudgy little hands around the thick tangle of honeysuckle and ivy, and began to shimmy up.

By the time the guard knight had spotted her, Grace was already halfway to the top.

At least she was heading towards an *empty* nest. The dragon it belonged to was out hunting. The others were dozing in their own turret-top nests, their great scaly tails wrapped around their treasures.

Even so, getting Grace down was a serious challenge. Climbing the tower was easy enough for a little girl, especially a brave and curious one like Grace. It was *not* so easy for a full-grown man in armour.

By the time the guard knight called for help, she'd managed to clamber right into the nest.

She seemed quite happy there, playing with jewels and coins. But if the dragon who'd collected them came *back* …

King Wonder himself ordered his entire band of knights to fetch the infant down. The men formed a human ladder that clanked … and clanged … and wobbled … but held fast as the bravest knight clambered to the top.

By the time he reached her, Grace was covered in coins and gemstones and dragons' toenails, stuck to her baby-soft skin by dragon poo.

Every single one of these things was said to bring good luck, even the poo. Judging by the state of her, Grace must be the luckiest girl in

the kingdom. At least that's what the knight said as he handed her gently over to the king.

And so it was that Grace came to live in Wondermere Castle. She was adopted by King Wonder himself and raised as a twin sister to the little Princess Portia.

Eight happy years passed. Princess Portia and Grace became best friends. Grace adored her sister and the king, who was the most wonderful father anyone could have wished for. Perhaps she really *was* the luckiest girl in the kingdom?

But she would happily have swapped her life of luxury for a unicorn and a suit of armour.

The knight who rescued her had made quite the impression. Such bravery. Such selflessness. Such *fun*.

Serving the king! Guarding the dragons! Riding a unicorn across the realm! Grace longed to do it all.

But that's where her luck ran out. She might not have known the rules when she *first* arrived at the castle, but she was all too familiar with them by now.

Girls DO NOT become knights.

2

GIRLS DO NOT BECOME KNIGHTS

'It's a stupid rule,' Grace said, taking a seat in the royal balcony. 'We'd make just as good knights as the boys.'

'We'd probably be better at playing troll-o too,' said Portia, sitting down as well.

'Not this again?' the king said. 'The Rules of Wondermere clearly state—'

Grace held up her fingers and began

making a list. 'Girls can't ride unicorns ...'

'Too risky,' her father agreed.

'Or wear armour ...'

'Too heavy.'

'We can't wield weapons ...'

'Absolutely not.'

'Or go on epic quests.'

The king frowned. 'How could you *possibly* go questing in a *dress*?!'

'We wouldn't *have to* if we were allowed to wear *trousers*,' said Portia.

Grace gave her sister a high five, then turned her attention to the troll-o pitch below.

The courtyard was filling up with young knights on unicorns. Half the boys wore red armour, the other blue. The two teams lined up beneath the royal box.

A boy in blue took off his helmet and bowed to the king. 'Permission to whack the troll, your majesty?'

'Permission granted, Sir Oliver!'

A boy in red lifted up his visor. 'M'ladies,' he said with a bow, 'I hope our manly sporting doth not overwhelm thee.'

Grace rolled her eyes. 'Thanks, Sir Arthur, but I'm sure we'll manage.'

She'd do more than manage. She'd follow every last twist, turn and whack of the troll, imagining *she* was playing too.

The ball-troll dashed across the cobbled pitch. It weaved between the unicorns' pounding hooves and ducked to avoid the knights' mallets.

Not that trolls minded being walloped. Their skin was so thick they barely felt a thing.

WHACK!

Grace applauded as a blur of fur went flying through the round goal hoop.

Every troll in the realm dreamed of becoming a ball-troll, just as every boy dreamed of becoming a knight.

Every boy and Princess Grace.

If only she were allowed to give troll-o a try. It would be the perfect practice for knighthood. It tested your strength, stamina, balance and skill. Although right now the boys weren't practising anything – they'd put down their mallets for a meadow-juice break.

A twinkle up among the clouds caught Grace's eye. A large purple dragon was returning to its nest, a blue gem glittering in its beak.

She watched as it landed with a thud, waking another dragon. The second dragon screeched, flapped its wings and flew lazily off over the surrounding treetops.

'The dear old things are getting excited,' said an elderly troll, waddling into the royal box. 'Only two weeks until Wondermere Day!'

Taffy Trafalgar was the king's oldest friend and closest advisor. He was also the girls' tutor. Grace sank lower in her seat. She'd much rather stay and watch the troll-o than face another day of princess lessons.

'I daresay they're looking forward to the celebrations,' the king said. 'How are the preparations going, Taffy?'

'All on track, sire,' the troll said, clicking

his furry heels together. 'Just the bunting to finish and we'll be all set. Come along, girls! Time for your sewing lesson.'

Grace groaned. 'Do we *have* to? They've just started goal practice!'

The boys were taking turns to try and whack the ball-troll through the goal hoop.

"THREE–NIL TO THE REDS!"

the ball-troll cried gleefully as it sailed past the royal box.

Taffy puffed out his chest. 'You most certainly *do* have to – the rules say so.

It won't take long. You've already sewn three thousand metres of the stuff. Just another seven thousand to go!'

Grace put her head in her hands, peeping out through a gap in her fingers so she didn't miss any goals.

'I don't see why we can't just fetch last year's bunting up from the dungeons and use it again?' Portia said. 'It's still in perfect condition.'

Taffy shook his head. 'That would never do.'

'Quite right, Taffy,' said the king, stroking his beard thoughtfully. 'We must stick to our rules and traditions. The aim of Wondermere Day is to *delight* the dragons, not *disturb* them.'

'I bet the dragons wouldn't care if we recycled last year's decorations,' Grace said, looking back up at the turret. The purple dragon had fallen asleep, ignoring the noise the knights were making down on the pitch.

Taffy shook his head, his long, rabbity ears flapping. 'Breaking the rules disturbs the dragons – and the rules quite clearly state that new bunting must be made *every year*!'

'The rules are stupid,' Grace said. Taffy gasped.

'The rules are vital,' King Wonder said, shaking his finger at Grace. 'They're there to protect us all. So long as the dragons remain in their nests, Wondermere will be blessed with good luck. We follow the rules for the sake of the realm. As a princess, you must set a good example.'

Grace scowled. 'I'd rather set an example with a mallet than a needle.'

'Me too,' Portia agreed. 'Anyway, we don't know *for sure* that breaking the rules would disturb the dragons. No one's ever studied them to find out. If we were allowed to get close enough to see …'

The king began to argue back, but Grace had stopped listening. The very thought of wielding a mallet had triggered a wonderful daydream.

She'd just scored the winning goal in the Wondermere Day Troll-o Tournament. The crowd was chanting her name as her father handed her the trophy, saying, *'Arise, Sir Grace! Champion of Champions! It's time for your sewing lesson!'*

'You what?!' Grace said, blinking.

'That bunting won't sew itself,' her father chuckled.

'You know what they say,' Taffy said, pulling her to her feet. '*A stitch a day helps the dragons to stay.*'

'Can we please watch just *one* more goal ... ?' Grace begged as her tutor tugged her towards the door.

The balcony was plunged briefly into shadow as a dragon flew directly overhead. Its belly gurgled like thunder. It had obviously eaten a lot of spangle moss that morning ...

SPLAT! Grace was covered in steaming poo.

'Eew!' she said, trying to wipe the runny mess from her shoulder. It was no use. Every last inch of her was covered in glittering dragon dung.

Portia gazed at her in awe. 'Amazing.'

'Remarkable,' Taffy said, adjusting his spectacles.

19

'Third time this week,' Grace said with a sigh.

Even the knights had stopped playing to put down their mallets and applaud. The king gazed at her proudly.

'See?' he said. 'You really *are* the luckiest girl in the kingdom!'

DO NOT STAND AT THE WRONG END OF A UNICORN

Grace and Portia spent three solid hours sewing. Two hundred metres of bunting later, they were finally free.

They headed straight for the stables to visit their friend Bram Bramwell, the young imp who took care of the royal unicorns.

Grace always felt at home in the castle stables. Bram was good company, and even if she wasn't allowed to *ride* a unicorn, there was no rule saying she couldn't *groom* one.

'Careful,' Bram said now. 'Leonard gets a bit *gassy* after playing troll-o.'

As if on cue, the unicorn Grace was brushing swished its silvery tail. A glittering cloud surrounded her.

'Smells like roses,' she said.

'Wait for it …' said Bram.

Grace started to cough. **'URGH!'**

She staggered around the stable, wafting her hands in front of her face. 'Rotten eggs!'

'There, there, Leonard,' said Portia, patting Leonard's long nose. 'Better out than in.'

Portia put her ear to the unicorn's belly. 'Sounds like a touch of pixie pox, actually. Try polishing his horn with witch wax, Bram. Should do the trick.'

'Thank you, Portia, I will,' Bram replied. 'You certainly know your unicorns.'

'It's all those books she reads,' Grace said.

Portia shrugged and began plaiting Leonard's mane. 'My books are OK, but getting up close to them in real life is *so* much better. I wish we could spend more time here in the stables. Magical creatures are the *best*.'

'You ought to visit my tree house,' Bram
said, shovelling up a pile of sparkling unicorn
poo. 'We get *wild* unicorns in our garden. Dad
loves them – collects their poo for his compost
heap.'

Grace wrinkled her nose. 'Eew!'

'That heap's my dad's pride and joy. Says it
puts luck into the earth. He even empties our
pet pop-weasel's litter tray into it.'

Portia sighed. 'Sounds like heaven.'

'The *compost heap*?!' Grace said.

'The *tree house*. And I can't believe you
have a pet pop-weasel! I've read about them,
but I've never seen one.'

'I've never seen one either,' Bram said.
'Wesley's really shy and can turn himself
invisible.'

Portia sighed. 'Your home sounds amazing.'

'Me and Dad would be delighted to have you, any time,' said Bram.

'If only,' Grace said, flopping down into a pile of straw. 'The rules won't let princesses leave the castle grounds!'

'The rules suck,' Portia said, feeding Leonard a cookie from her dress pocket.

'They really do,' Grace agreed. 'I'm supposed to be *the luckiest girl in the kingdom.* How lucky is it to be cooped up in a castle your whole life? Seriously, Bram – do I look lucky to you?'

'I wasn't going to mention it, but you look kind of *poopy* today, actually ...'

'Exactly,' Grace said, getting back to her feet. 'There's no such thing as luck. I'm covered in poo, I'm not allowed to wash it off because it's supposed to bring good fortune,

25

I had to spend the whole morning sewing – and now I'm covered in unicorn fart!'

Just at that moment, Leonard's bottom let out another glittering cloud. Grace's shoulders sagged.

Bram laughed. 'That's lucky too!'

Grace dropped back down on to the straw. Portia joined her.

'Don't the rules get on *your* nerves?' Grace asked Bram.

'It must be annoying,' Portia agreed, 'not

being allowed to be a knight just because you're an imp.'

'I've never really *wanted* to be a knight,' Bram said with a shrug. 'Although if I ever fancied giving it a try, I could just use my magic to transform into one. No one would know the difference. Dad's been giving me shape-shifting lessons. Watch this – one knight, coming up!'

Bram put down his shovel, frowned in concentration, clapped his hands together … and turned into an armchair.

'Nice one, Bram,' Grace laughed, taking

a seat on her friend. 'That straw was getting uncomfortable!'

CLAP! The chair disappeared from under her and turned back into the young imp. 'All that sword-and-shield stuff doesn't interest me anyway. I'd sooner be a princess, to be honest.'

Grace's eyes widened. 'But being a princess *sucks*! Being an imp must be loads better?'

'Not really. I'd rather live in a castle than the woods any day,' Bram said. 'I mean, our tree house is *nice* and everything, but it doesn't have any dragons nesting on it – and there are no banisters to slide down.'

'What use are banisters when you're wearing all these petticoats?' Grace complained.

'I quite like the petticoats,' Portia said,

getting to her feet to pet Leonard.

'Well, *I'd* prefer armour,' Grace said. She grabbed an empty bucket, put it on her head, swung her leg over a broom and trotted off around the stable.

'All hail Sir Grace,' she cried, 'guardian of the dragons, ten-times troll-o champion, bravest knight in all Wondermere!'

Portia followed suit, using Bram's shovel as a unicorn. Bram joined in too, taking the part of the ball-troll.

'Whack me if you can!' he called, dodging the girls as they charged after him.

Grace snatched up a broom, swinging it around like a troll-o mallet. **'WALLOP!'** she cried, smacking Bram on the bottom.

'GOAL,' Portia yelled, 'and the crowd goes wild!'

The excitement was too much for Leonard.
The stable was filled with glitter.

'Ouch!' Bram said, rubbing his bottom.
'Nice shot. Now it's your turn to be the troll!'

He took the broom from Grace and
cantered off around the stable.

'It's a good job we're not allowed to play for
real,' Portia giggled. 'Those boys would never
know what hit them!'

Portia trotted off after Bram, but Grace gazed blankly after them. She tugged the bucket further down on to her head until her face was hidden completely.

'You're right,' she said to herself, voice muffled by the bucket. 'They'd never know *at all*!'

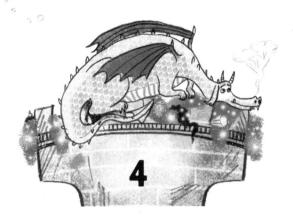

GIRLS DO NOT
WEAR TROUSERS

Grace and Portia arrived super early for their sewing lesson the next day. They concentrated hard and finished the Wondermere Day bunting in record time.

By lunchtime, row upon row of neat triangles were ready to hang between the castle turrets, each flag embroidered with huge gold letters.

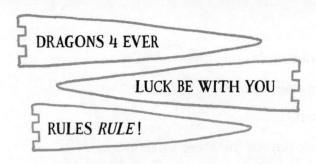

DRAGONS 4 EVER

LUCK BE WITH YOU

RULES *RULE*!

'I knew you loved sewing really,' Taffy said, watching proudly as Grace put the last stitch in her final metre of bunting. 'Your work is complete, girls! You're free to visit the stables.'

Grace grinned. Finishing early was all part of her plan.

'Actually, Taffy,' she said slyly, 'we'd like to stay awhile longer and sew Dad some new Under-Wonders ...'

'Special full-length ones for Wondermere Day,' Portia added, 'to bring him luck.'

Taffy hopped up and down in delight. 'Go ahead, girls, what a kind gesture. *Every* man deserves some extra comfort beneath his armour on Wondermere Day.'

So does every girl ... Grace thought to herself.

Her tongue poked out in concentration as her Under-Wonders came together, the golden thread she'd chosen glowing in the light of the setting sun. By the time she'd finished sewing, the dragons were settling down for the night.

Grace put down her needle and held the Under-Wonders against her waist. 'Perfect!'

Portia held her own pink pair up for size.

'Er, I don't like to criticise, girls,' Taffy said, tugging anxiously at his ears, 'but aren't they a little *small* for your father?'

'Oh well, it's the thought that counts,' Grace said, stuffing her pair into her dress pocket.

'You're absolutely right, princess,' Taffy said. 'I'm sure his majesty will appreciate your efforts.' The old troll yawned and stretched.

Outside the window, the nearest dragon followed suit, stretching out its great wings, tucking them against its sides and closing its eyes.

'Off to bed, girls,' Taffy said, gently herding the girls out of the classroom. 'You've worked super hard today.'

Grace smiled as she waved him goodnight. She knew the *real* hard work was only just beginning.

With Wondermere Day coming up, all the knights-in-training were still out in the courtyard for extra troll-o practice. Even so, it was best to move quickly.

'If we're going to secretly learn how to play troll-o, we'll be needing more than just Under-Wonders,' Grace said, leading the way to the royal armour store.

'Are you sure the boys won't notice there's some armour missing?' Portia said as they slipped cautiously inside the storeroom.

'No chance,' Grace said, closing the door quietly behind them. 'This stuff's all old and damaged.' She pulled a breastplate out from the pile and slipped it on over her dress. 'See? It's all dented.'

Portia frowned. 'Doesn't that mean it's no good?'

Grace shrugged. 'We can fix it up. Bang the dents back out, polish it up a bit … It'll be good enough. Anyway, it's not as though we need to look good. No one's ever going to *see* us wearing it!'

'They'd better not,' Portia giggled. 'We'd be in *massive* trouble if they did.'

'There's no harm, we're only playing dress-up.' Grace put on a helmet and flipped the visor down over her face. 'How do I look?'

Portia grinned. 'Totally cool.'

Sneaking into the armoury was one thing, but sneaking back out again was quite another. It isn't easy to walk with a full suit of armour hidden under your skirts.

'At least we finally found a use for all these petticoats,' Grace joked as they clanked along the candlelit corridors to their bedroom. 'Who knew you could hide so much cool stuff underneath them?'

'Hail, princesses!'

'Oh, no!' squealed Portia, clutching Grace's arm. Sir Arthur and Sir Oliver were coming down the corridor towards them.

'*Act normal*,' Grace hissed.

'Greetings, m'ladies,' said Sir Arthur with a low bow. 'May we assist you in some way, forsooth?'

'No thanks,' Grace said, 'but if you don't stop speaking like that, *I* may flickest thee on the nose, forsooth.'

Sir Oliver blushed. 'Forgive us. 'Tis the rules for knights to speaketh this way.' He

cleared his throat, clicked his heels together and saluted. '*A rule a day helps the dragons to stay!*'

'If you say so,' Grace said.

'Aren't you boys meant to be at extra troll-o practice?' Portia asked.

'The dragons are looking twitchy,' Sir Arthur said. 'The king thinks someone must be breaking the rules. He sent us to investigate.'

'Crikey,' Portia said, shooting a nervous look at Grace.

'I doubt anyone's doing anything wrong,' Grace said. 'The dragons are probably fidgety because *you lot* keep practising troll-o every minute of the day.'

Sir Oliver shook his head. ''Tis tradition to play extra matches in preparation for Wondermere Day. We must be at our best to honour the dragons – and we shall honour them now by catching the rule breakers!'

Portia let out a nervous squeak.

Sir Arthur gave her a concerned look. 'Do not be afraid! No harm shall befall thee when we're around – **EEK!**' He took a flying leap backwards and pointed to the floor at Grace's feet.

Grace held her breath. Had he spotted the stolen armour poking out beneath her skirts?

'**DIRT!**' he cried. 'Do not spoil thy dainty slippers!'

Grace let out a sigh of relief. He hadn't seen a thing.

Sir Oliver whipped off his cloak and laid it at the girls' feet. 'Rule number thirty-seven,' he said. '**DO NOT abandon a damsel in distress!**'

'But *you're* the ones distressing us,' Grace said.

Portia fixed a smile on her face. 'Come on, Grace, let's get our dainty selves to bed.'

The girls linked arms – not easy when you're concealing a troll-o mallet up your sleeve – and stepped around the cloak.

CLANG!

'W-what was that?!' Sir Arthur said, clinging to Sir Oliver in panic. His eyes roved the corridor, searching for a hidden enemy. Sir Oliver drew his sword.

'*I* didn't hear anything,' said Grace, faking a yawn. 'We really *must* get to bed ...'

TING!!

'There it was again!' Sir Arthur cried. 'A most fearsome clatter! Perhaps 'tis the *rule breakers*?!'

43

'Um ...' Portia said, looking to Grace for help.

'Oh, you mean *that* sound?' Grace said, shaking a leg and setting her armour rattling. 'It's my, er ... lucky cans of dragon poop.'

'Your *what*?' said Sir Oliver, screwing up his nose.

'You know how they're always pooping on me? *Luckiest girl in the kingdom* and all that. I keep some of it. Carry a few cans of it with me for *extra* luck.'

'She's given me some too,' Portia said, shaking her leg with a clatter. 'Poop-in-a-can! You can't beat it.'

'Poop-in-a-can?' Sir Oliver looked impressed. ''Tis a most generous gift.'

Grace gave a saintly smile. 'Generosity is my middle name.'

'I say,' Sir Oliver said, leaning in and whispering, 'you couldn't spare a little poop for me?'

'Cheat!' Sir Arthur cried. 'You just want an advantage on Wondermere Day!'

Sir Oliver looked offended. 'An outrageous suggestion. I was merely thinking of our quest to find the rule breakers. With lucky poop on our side we might find them faster.'

Grace gave a half-hearted curtsy. 'Very noble of you. I'd be *delighted* to give you a can – but not right now. I need to go to bed.'

Portia yawned, genuinely this time. 'Us girls need our beauty sleep.'

'Sleep tight,' Grace called over her shoulder as she and Portia clanked down the corridor. 'Don't let the dragons take flight!'

5

DO NOT STAY
UP ALL NIGHT

You can't run a kingdom on a poor night's
sleep. By ten o'clock that night, King Wonder
was tucked up in bed.

His subjects snoozed too, dozing in cottages,
farms, huts and burrows throughout the
realm. Grace and Portia were the only two
people in the castle still awake – astonishing
given the racket they were making.

The armour was in need of an oil. Their homemade Under-Wonders made it a little less uncomfortable, but it still creaked and clanked with every move.

'We'll have more space to play if we push our beds against the walls,' Grace said, dragging her four-poster noisily across the flagstones.

'Good idea,' Portia said, lending a hand.

'That's better,' Grace said. 'Let's do this!' She jumped on to her bed and swung her mallet.

'Oops!' said Portia, ducking. 'There go my books!'

'There's not enough room to swing a pixie in here,' Grace grumbled.

'We'll just have to make the best of it,' Portia said, putting her books back on the shelf. 'And I s'pose we ought to shut the window so we don't disturb the dragons.'

'How are they looking?' Grace asked.

Portia popped her head out of the open window. 'Hmm … you'd better come and see.'

Grace clanked across the room and took a look. The ancient beasts were grumbling and griping in their nests.

'Maybe the boys were right,' Portia said. 'They're certainly making a lot more fuss than normal.'

'I'm sure they're fine,' Grace said, pulling the window shut. 'They probably *always* do this, only we never normally see because we're fast asleep.'

'I guess so,' Portia said with a shrug. 'Fancy a match, then?'

'First to three,' Grace said, grabbing a doll from her pillow. 'Mrs Muggins volunteers to be the ball-troll.'

'Thanks, Mrs Muggins,' said Portia. She swung her mallet, sent the toy flying – then gave a little shriek of panic. Her arms were fixed in place, pointing up at the vaulted ceiling above her head. 'My armour's rusted into place!'

'Bummer,' Grace said. 'You can't play troll-o with your arms stuck in the air.'

'I can't do *anything* with my arms stuck in the air – including taking this stuff off!'

'You can't be *properly* stuck,' Grace said, clanking over to help her sister. She raised her own arms to help – but *they* jammed in place too. 'Oh, ogre bogeys!'

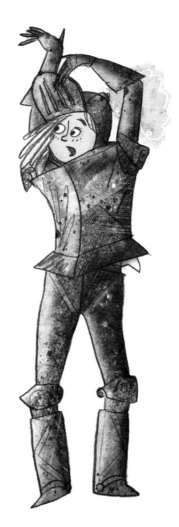

Portia's voice went high with panic. 'We can't still be like this in the morning! *Princesses DO NOT wear armour!*'

'But on the bright side,' Grace said, 'we'll be *awesome* at musical statues.'

'That's not funny!' Portia looked as though she might cry – then her face lit up. 'Troll spit!'

'Same to you,' Grace said.

'No, we *need* troll spit! I read about it in one of my books – it's what the knights use to oil their armour. Trolls have oil glands under their tongues. *Super greasy.*'

Grace pulled a face. 'But where are we going to get hold of troll spit in the middle of the night?'

The girls shared a look, then said together, 'Taffy Trafalgar!'

DO NOT WAKE
A SLEEPING TROLL

Aside from a few enchanted gargoyles who gave the girls some very funny looks, the girls managed to get to Taffy's room without waking anyone.

By the time they'd clattered down the corridors their knees had rusted stiff. They shuffled into his room in a series of noisy hops, closing the door behind them.

In spite of the racket, their tutor was still sleeping soundly, curled up on a bed made of solid rock.

'Yowch,' Grace said. 'I'm glad I'm not a troll.'

Portia shrugged. 'Comfiest thing for all that tough skin.'

'WHACK!' Taffy yelled suddenly, making both girls jump. Grace calmed down when she realised his eyes were still tightly shut.

'It's OK,' she said, heart still thudding inside her armour. 'He's talking in his sleep. Sounds like he's dreaming about his troll-o playing days – listen.'

'Can't catch me, Sir Slowcoach! Wheeee!'

Portia giggled. But there was no time to stand around watching their tutor relive his youth.

'Wake up,' Grace said firmly. 'By order of the king!'

'Yes, Mummy! I mean, yes, Sir Wotsit-chops!' Taffy fell off his rock and landed on the floor. He rubbed his eyes sleepily and peered up at the girls. 'What's going on? Is that *you*, Sir Hector?'

'It so totally *is*,' said a gruff voice.

It so totally *wasn't*, but Grace was doing a pretty good job of sounding manly.

Portia followed suit, making her voice as deep as she could. 'His majesty's men need your spit.'

Grace thrust her armpits towards Taffy. 'Cough up for king and country!'

'Is that … Sir Derek?'

'I expect so,' Portia said.

Taffy frowned. The girls had managed to

flip their visors down to hide their faces. It hadn't been easy without the use of their hands – they'd had to knock their heads against their chamber door until the visors fell into place.

'Why are you pointing to the ceiling?' Taffy asked.

'Our armour's rusted stiff,' Grace said. 'Now will you please hurry up and spit on our armpits – king's orders!'

'I'm not sure I can manage any spit right now, sir,' Taffy said, smacking his lips together. 'Terribly dry mouth.' He yawned and his eyelids began to droop. 'I slibble a lot in my dreep ...'

'He's falling asleep standing up!' Grace groaned.

'Wake up,' Portia pleaded, 'we need you!'

'Three—nil! Threeeee—nil!' Taffy sang.

Grace poked the troll with an armoured toe. He let out a rattling snore.

'Now what?!' Portia said.

'OK, I have an idea,' Grace said, bracing herself. 'I need you to shove me on to his pillow, head first.'

Portia looked at her blankly. 'You do realise his pillow is made of *solid rock*?'

'And covered in troll spit,' Grace said. 'Look – he really *does* dribble a lot in his sleep.'

'Eew!'

'There's plenty there for both of us, but I'm so stiff I can't reach it,' Grace said. 'If I could just connect my *armpits* with it ...'

'Say no more,' said Portia. She shuffled stiffly up to her sister and bumped into her, hard.

Unable to use her arms to stop herself, Grace fell face first towards Taffy's rock bed. 'Bullseye!' Her armpits had landed right on slimy target.

She began to move her arms around, stiffly at first, then more and more freely as the spit did its work. She dipped her armoured fingertips into the little puddle of drool and rubbed it into her knee joints. Then she stood up and began rubbing it into Portia's armour.

'What a relief,' Portia said, swinging her arms in wide circles. 'I was getting *terrible* pins and needles.'

'*Terrible pins and needles*,' Taffy said suddenly. 'You must work harder at your embroidery!'

The girls froze, but the troll's eyes were still closed.

'Out like a light,' Portia whispered.

'Good,' Grace said. 'Let's make the most of this spit. We might as well give our whole suits the once-over while we're here ...'

They kept one eye on Taffy as they worked. The creaks and cranks quickly quietened, and the girls slipped out in silence, leaving their tutor dreaming.

DO NOT LIE
TO THE KING

'It's the strangest thing,' Taffy Trafalgar said, taking a seat at the breakfast table. 'I woke up this morning *standing up.*'

'Gosh,' Grace said, 'I wonder how that happened?' Portia stifled a giggle.

'I've absolutely no idea,' Taffy said, blinking sleepily. 'I was in the middle of the oddest dream about knights' armpits ...'

'Sounds like you've been working too hard,' Grace said, helping herself to a fifth slice of toast. 'Perhaps you should take the day off. Don't you think so, Dad?'

The king looked up from his porridge. 'It's not a bad idea. You said the girls have completed the bunting?'

'Everything's ready for Wondermere Day,' Taffy said, rubbing his eyes. 'They've even finished your new Under-Wonders.'

'They were supposed to be a secret!' Portia said, putting down her book.

'You made me Under-Wonders?' the king said with a smile. 'How kind! May I see them?'

'They're too small,' Grace said, spreading honey on her sixth slice of toast. 'Anyway, the rules say it's bad luck to see them before Wondermere Day.'

The king chuckled. 'I thought you didn't *believe* in luck?'

Before Grace could answer, Taffy landed face first in his porridge, blowing bubbles as he let out a huge snore.

'All the preparation's tired him out,' the king said, easing Taffy gently out of his breakfast. 'You girls are quite right. He deserves a day off.'

'Serve an off day,' Taffy babbled, falling straight back into his food.

'If we don't have any lessons,' Grace said, 'could we go and see if Bram needs any help?'

The king tugged thoughtfully at his beard. 'Very well – but only as far as the stables. No sneaking out of the castle grounds!'

'Thanks, Dad!' Grace gave him a hug.

The king smiled. 'Give young master Bramwell my regards. The unicorns are looking splendid.'

The girls skipped the whole way to the stables, Grace chewing on yet another slice of toast. She gave the crust to Leonard, who was freshly groomed and gleaming, ready for a day's troll-o practice.

He chewed the crust, raised a silver eyebrow in pleasure … and released a cloud of glitter from his rear end.

Grace put her hands over her nose and held her breath.

'No need to worry. I used witch wax, like Portia suggested,' Bram said, strolling round from the neighbouring stall. 'Leonard still farts, but now they smell of roses. I used it on *all* the unicorns in the end. Bought a huge can of it at the forest market.'

'They all look amazing,' Portia said, 'and the stables smell *much* nicer.'

'It's all thanks to you,' Bram said.

Portia smiled, tried to curtsy – then gave up. After breakfast she and Grace had stopped by their chamber and hidden their armour beneath their skirts again.

Bram frowned. 'Looks like you could use some witch wax too.'

Portia giggled.

'Not quite – but we *could* use a favour in return,' Grace said, giving Bram a cheeky smile.

His eyes narrowed. 'It doesn't involve breaking the rules, does it?'

Grace grinned. 'Only a couple of *teensy-weensy* ones ...'

8

PRINCESSES DO NOT LEAVE THE CASTLE GROUNDS

The woods surrounding Wondermere Castle were most perilous for a princess.

She might snag her skirts on some brambles, get mud on her slippers or get jinxed by a leprechaun.

Grace really hoped she might – although so far the only magical creatures she'd seen were the clouds of wood nymphs

67

buzzing around her face.

'Blimey,' Grace said as they whizzed past, 'I reckon they're even more excited than me!'

Bram smiled. 'They're not used to seeing princesses in the forest.'

Portia kept her voice low as they headed deeper into the trees. 'Are you sure no one saw us sneaking out?'

'Don't worry,' Bram said, 'me and Dad are the only ones who use the back entrance to the stables. Anyway, if anyone *does* see us I'll just shape-shift and turn myself into a mumblebee. You two could pretend you were chasing me and just lost track of where you were.'

'Can imps really change into mumblebees?' Grace asked.

'Probably,' Bram said.

'But mumblebees are *tiny*,' Portia said, impressed.

'I've been practising – watch!' Bram clapped his hands together and turned into … a wheelbarrow.

Grace laughed. 'A lesser spotted wheely-bee!'

'I'll try again,' the wheelbarrow said, rocking from side to side.

'No, stay like that,' Grace said, 'you'll be useful.'

She and Portia reached beneath their skirts, pulling out pieces of heavy armour and dropping them into the barrow with a **CLANG!**

'Crikey,' Bram said, 'that stuff's heavier than it looks!'

'You should try carrying it around in your

underwear,' Portia complained.

'Stop grumbling, you two,' Grace said. 'We've only got three hours before the knights finish troll-o practice. They'll expect you to be back in the stables when they're done.'

'Dad will be wondering where *we* are by then too,' Portia said, reaching out to let a pixie land on her finger.

Grace took Bram's handles and let him lead the way to a wide clearing. 'Here we are,' he said. 'Home sweet home!'

He turned back to his impish self, the armour rattling to the floor in a heap.

Grace's eyes sparkled with pleasure as she took in Bram's enchanting home. It couldn't be more different to Wondermere Castle.

There were no neat stone walls, just beautiful tangles of leaves and wild flowers, all covered in pixie dust and sparkling in the sunlight. A family of fairies came out of their toadstool house to get a good look at the girls.

'Is that a goblin burrow over there?' Portia gasped. 'And is that a boggart nest? Ooh, a marshmallow tree!'

'That tree is my house,' Bram said proudly. 'Hey, Dad, I'm home – and I brought visitors!'

The pink, puffy tree trunk lit up with twinkling lights, revealing a door and several windows that stretched right the way to the top. The door opened and an older version of Bram stepped through it.

'Hello, son!' He welcomed Bram with a hug, then spotted the princesses. 'Oh my giddy goblins! If I knew we were expecting royalty I'd have washed – I've been tending to my compost heap all morning.' He waved a hand towards an enormous pile beside the tree.

'Wow,' Grace said, trying not to look disgusted. The dark, steaming mountain buzzed with flies. 'Impressive.'

'Thank you,' Bram's dad said, his chest swelling with pride.

'The princesses need our help,' Bram

explained to his father. 'Grace, Portia – this is my dad, Bunkum.'

Bunkum bowed.

'It's a pleasure to meet you,' Grace said.

Portia threw her arms around him. 'Bram's told us so much about you! What a lovely home you have! Are there *really* wild unicorns in your garden?'

Bunkum chuckled, waving a hand towards the clearing. 'They like to graze on the fallen marshmallows. Greedy blighters.'

Portia bent down and examined the floor. 'Fresh hoof prints!'

'The girls want to learn to play troll-o,' Bram said. 'They're hoping we might help them tame a couple of wild unicorns, seeing as they're not allowed trained ones like the king's men.'

'Girls playing troll-o?' Bunkum raised his eyebrows. 'That would be against the rules...'

Grace's shoulders drooped, but Bunkum laughed, clapped his hands together – and turned into a squashy sofa.

'Those silly old rules aren't worth the parchment they're written on,' the sofa said. 'Grace, Bram – take a seat. Princess Portia is about to meet her steed!'

9

DO NOT USE
NAUGHTY WORDS

Grace perched on one of Bunkum's comfortable arms. Her face was beginning to ache from smiling so widely. It was hard to believe this was actually *happening*. She was just minutes away from riding a real live unicorn!

Her sister was standing in the middle of the clearing, following Bram and Bunkum's instructions.

'List all the loveliest things you can think of,' Bram said.

'And don't forget to close your eyes,' the sofa added.

Portia squeezed her eyes shut and threw her arms to the sky. 'Libraries! Troll babies! Freshly laundered pyjamas! A delicious mug of steaming hot chocolate!'

Just as Portia finished her list, a wild unicorn appeared at the edge of the clearing. Grace held her breath. It looked just like a cup of hot chocolate – its legs were a warm brown, its back was white as whipped cream, and its mane and tail were flecked with rainbow sprinkles.

'Bravo, princess!' said the sofa.

'Steady now,' said Bram. 'Arms out in front of you, palms up.'

Portia did as she was told, keeping her eyes tightly closed. Grace bit her lip and tried not to fidget. She could hardly wait for her turn.

She watched as the unicorn approached Portia cautiously, then laid its muzzle gently in her hands.

'Time to name him,' Bram said quietly. 'Keep your eyes closed until you've said it!'

'I think I'll call you ... *Sprinkles*!' Portia

said. She opened her eyes and squealed with delight. 'He's **SPRINKLY!**'

Bram grinned and gave Portia a double thumbs up.

'Portia, how did you *know*?' Grace gasped.

'It's all part of the magic,' Bram grinned.

'Your turn, Princess Grace,' said the sofa.

Portia beamed at her sister. 'Good luck!'

Grace took a deep breath and walked to the centre of the clearing. Her stomach felt like it was filled with a thousand jittery pixies.

'Close your eyes and think happy thoughts,' Bram said.

Grace squeezed her eyes shut and tried her best to recall one of her favourite daydreams.

She was seated on a gleaming, golden-haired unicorn, receiving the Wondermere Day troll-o trophy from the king. '*You are the most awesome knight EVER,*' he said.

'Now list your loveliest things,' Bunkum said. 'Speak nice and clearly!'

A grin spread across her face. 'Knights! Armour! Troll-o! Daring deeds and epic quests!'

'Eyes shut!' Bram ordered.

Grace was so tempted to peep. Bunkum was whispering something, then she heard Portia gasp. There was a faint rustle from the trees.

Could it be her unicorn? Yes – surely those were hoof steps she heard now, crunching cautiously closer ... and closer ...

'Hands out, palms up,' Bram said quietly.

Grace hardly dared to breathe. At last she felt warm breath tickling her fingertips. Her heart soared.

'Time to name him,' Bram said quietly.

Grace couldn't wait to open her eyes and meet her unicorn properly. What would he look like? A great, golden beauty with silver hair and a glittering horn! He'd need a dignified name to suit.

Grace wracked her brain. Perhaps something strong like Gloryblade? Or maybe something glamorous, like Glitterbug?

'I name you ...' she began.

Her eyes were still clamped tightly shut, so she didn't notice the shadow passing above her as a dragon flew high overhead.

SPLAT!

'... *POOP?!*' Grace spluttered. 'Ugh! Oh, no. What have I done?!'

'You've tamed a wild unicorn,' Bunkum said. 'Congratulations!'

Grace wiped the dragon dung from her face. 'But I named him Poop!'

'You sure did,' Bram said, coming over to join her, 'and it suits him.'

Before her stood a grubby, mottled beast with a tangled mane and a horn the colour of dishwater. It swished its tail at the flies buzzing around its bottom.

'He's, erm ... not quite what I expected,' Grace said, sounding a little disappointed.

Bram laughed. 'He's amazing – and so are you. You did it!'

'I did, didn't I?' Grace broke into a wide grin. 'I tamed a wild unicorn!'

'And got covered in dragon poo at the same time,' Portia said, looking Grace up and down. 'You really are *so* lucky.'

'So am *I*,' said Bunkum, changing back to normal with a clap. 'Fresh poo for my lucky compost heap!' He set about scooping the mess into a bucket.

Grace couldn't stop smiling. 'My very own unicorn! Nice to meet you, Poop.'

Poop sneezed, covering her with green snot, then he looked her up and down, disgusted. Grace couldn't help but laugh.

'Did you see what that dragon was carrying just now?' Portia asked Bram. 'It looked like boring old grub moss.'

'Yes, I noticed that,' Bram said, sounding concerned. He looked to the sky but the dragon was long gone. 'Very odd. Grub moss isn't sparkly *at all.*'

Portia turned to Grace. 'Maybe something really *is* disturbing the dragons?'

Grace shrugged, giving all her attention to Poop, who was busy trying to bite her ankles. 'They're fine – and there's certainly nothing wrong with that one's *aim.*'

'Well done, girls,' Bunkum said, dumping a fresh pail of poo into his glittering heap. 'You did it! That took determination and strength of mind – vital skills for any knight.'

Grace grinned. 'Thanks so much for your help!'

'Oh, it was nothing,' the old imp said, wiping his hands on his tunic. 'Now: if you're going to learn to play troll-o, I daresay you'll be needing a ball-troll ... ?'

He clapped his hands together and turned into one. 'Can't catch me!' he said, bouncing off around the clearing.

'Maybe we shouldn't be doing this?' Portia said. 'I mean, if the dragons really *are* disturbed ... ?'

'Forget it,' Grace said, 'all *you* need to worry about is me scoring more goals than you. Last one in their armour's a baby bog-bubbler!'

GIRLS DO NOT
RIDE UNICORNS

The girls didn't have long left to practise –
but Portia and Sprinkles didn't *need* long.

'Wheee!' Portia cried, letting go of
Sprinkles's mane. She flung her arms out
wide, not even wobbling as he cantered
effortlessly after ball-troll Bunkum.

Grace and Poop weren't getting along quite
so well. Bram tried helping them, but he soon

backed off when Poop tried to bite him on the
bottom.

'He won't do anything I want him to,'
Grace complained as Poop stopped to graze
on a patch of bog wart.

She was close to tears. She'd done
everything Bram suggested, but Poop *would
not* do as she asked. 'He's just so *stubborn.*'

Bram laughed. 'Remind you of anyone?'

Grace scowled. 'I am *not* stubborn! I just don't like following the rules.'

'Neither does Poop, I guess,' said Bram with a shrug. 'Unicorns tend to be a lot like their riders. You two'll have to figure out how to get along if you're serious about learning to play troll-o.'

Grace gritted her teeth and flipped down her visor. 'I'm *super* serious – and I don't just want to *practise*. I want to be the best knight there ever was.'

'Then you'd better get a move on,' Bunkum said, whizzing past in a green blur. 'I just heard the half-time bell from the castle courtyard.'

'Come on, Poop,' Bram said, 'just an hour more, then we'll leave you alone.'

Poop ignored him and carried on chewing.

Grace tugged firmly on his mane. 'Stop eating and chase the ball-troll.'

Bram laughed. 'He's doing the opposite of what you say just to spite you!'

'Oh yeah? Two can play at that game.' Grace leaned down and spoke firmly in Poop's ear. 'Eat *more*,' she ordered. 'Do as I say and stuff your face. I *love it* when you stand around chewing.'

She felt her new steed tense beneath her. Then he snorted, stomped a hoof and spat out his food.

'Oh, no! He's stopped eating,' Grace said theatrically. 'I'm *so* disappointed. I really hope he doesn't canter around the clearing next ...'

Poop bounded off, falling neatly into stride with Sprinkles.

'HA!' Grace cried in triumph. 'He's doing it! Don't stop, Poop! Oops! I mean—'

Poop stopped in his tracks – but Grace kept going. She flew straight off his back and crashed into a tree.

'Are you OK?' Portia said, trotting neatly over on Sprinkles.

'I'm fine,' Grace huffed, pulling twigs and leaves out of her visor.

Bram dashed over to help her up. 'It's OK, I've got this,' she said, straightening her armour. '*Don't* come and rescue me, Poop.'

Looking terribly pleased with himself, Poop trotted disobediently to Grace's side. She winked at Bram before giving Poop his next order. 'Don't stand still while I mount you.'

Poop stood as still as a statue. Even his flies seemed to stop buzzing as Grace swung an armoured leg over his broad back.

'Definitely stand here for ages. Don't trot off round the clearing after the ball-troll. And *please* throw me off again? I *love it* when you do that.'

Poop sneered, then trotted obediently after Bunkum. 'I do believe she's cracked it,' the old imp laughed, mimicking a ball-troll perfectly as he darted in and out of Poop's pounding hooves.

Bram smiled. 'Well, if you two don't need an instructor, perhaps I can make myself useful as a goal?'

CLAP! He turned into a laundry basket. 'I suppose it'll do,' he sighed.

Once she'd got the hang of it, troll-o practice was everything Grace had dreamed it would be. The thunder of hooves! The swish of swinging mallets! The thrill of the chase!

She leaned forward in the saddle, mallet swinging.

WHACK! Bunkum flew straight into Bram's makeshift goal. 'She shoots, she scores!' Grace yelled, punching the air in triumph.

Even Poop seemed pleased with himself as

he swished his grubby horn round in celebration.

Sprinkles trotted over. Portia leaned out of the saddle and gave Grace a high five. 'That was amazing!'

'You're a natural,' said Bunkum,

clambering out of the laundry basket goal. Bram applauded loudly, accidentally turning himself into a teapot, a water fountain and then a grandfather clock.

Grace beamed with pleasure as she rode off around the clearing. Her armour was beginning to feel like a second skin. Even riding Poop was easy now she knew how to control him.

Bunkum was right – acting like a knight really *did* come naturally to her. Perhaps it was time to set her sights on a bigger target…

11

DO NOT STAY IN THE BATH UNTIL YOUR SKIN GOES WRINKLY

The girls left the unicorns grazing beneath the Bramwells' tree house. Bunkum had been very happy to keep an eye on them – their dung would be a welcome addition to his compost heap.

He'd told the girls to leave their armour with him too. It would save them carrying it back and forth every time they sneaked

out of the castle to practise.

'I'll fix it up for you in my spare time,'
Bram said as he led them back to the castle.

They crossed the moat bridge and slipped
into the back door to the stables just in time.
The knights were trooping tiredly in from
the courtyard. Bram got straight to work
unsaddling the unicorns while the boys
clanked off to the royal baths for a soak.

'Do you *have* any spare time?' Grace asked.

Bram smiled. 'A little. Don't worry. Working on your armour will make a nice change from shovelling poo. Hadn't you two better go? Your dad will be wondering where you are.'

'I s'pose,' Grace said reluctantly. 'Thanks for everything, Bram.'

'Thanks to your dad too,' Portia added. 'You imps are the best.'

The girls left Bram unsaddling the royal unicorns and traipsed tiredly off towards their bedroom.

'I hope Bram gets a rest soon.' Grace yawned. 'I could use one too.'

'You could use a bath first,' Portia laughed.

Grace looked down at her filthy dress.

She'd had so much fun playing troll-o, she'd forgotten she was covered in unicorn sneeze and dragon dung. 'I'm not going to the royal baths now, they'll be too crowded,' she said. 'Come on, let's go and take a dip in the moat.'

Grace left her dirty clothes on the drawbridge and jumped into the moat in her vest and bloomers. The warm, silvery waters washed the last traces of dirt from her skin as she swam lazily between the frillypads, leaving a trail of sparkling dung behind her.

A thoroughly disgusted mermaid swam quickly away in the opposite direction. 'Sorry!' Grace called after her.

'You really know how to spread your good luck around,' Portia laughed, lowering herself carefully into the water to get a closer look at a water sprite.

Grace was floating happily on her back, lost in a daydream, when a loud voice cried, 'Hail, good ladies!'

Sir Oliver and Sir Arthur were passing over the drawbridge, both freshly scrubbed and in their pyjamas. 'Be careful in there, princesses,' said Sir Arthur seriously. 'Too much water can be most vexatious.'

'Rule number two hundred and two,' Sir Oliver quoted, '**DO NOT stay in the bath until your skin goes wrinkly.**'

'Haven't you boys got anything better to do than spout rules at princesses?' Grace said, pulling herself out of the water to sit on the edge of the drawbridge.

'Yeah,' added Portia, treading water,

'I thought you were meant to be seeking out our dad's *mysterious rule breakers*?'

'Exactly why we're patrolling the castle walls,' said Sir Arthur proudly. 'His majesty is right to worry. The dragons are *definitely* unhappy.'

'Oh?' Grace wrung the water out of her hair and looked up at the turret tops. The nests *were* looking rather ragged.

'They've been kicking all the jewels out,' Sir Oliver said, stooping down and picking a small emerald up from the ground. 'See? Someone's obviously breaking rules – and breaking them *badly*.'

Grace shrugged and began gathering up her dirty clothes. 'The dragon probably just dropped it by accident.'

Sir Oliver shook his head. 'This is no

accident. They've clearly gone off glitter.'

Sir Arthur's voice wobbled with emotion. 'Some kind of change is bothering them. They could even be preparing to leave.'

Portia looked horrified. She pulled herself out of the moat and stood dripping beside Grace. 'Me and Bram saw one carrying grub moss earlier. Maybe there really *is* a problem?'

Grace waved a hand dismissively. 'I expect they finally figured out that grub moss is softer than gemstones. Wouldn't *you* want a bit of comfort after sleeping on a bed of jagged jewels for centuries?'

'But jewels are *lucky*,' said Sir Oliver, giving Grace's pile of dirty clothes a jealous look. 'Speaking of luck, I don't suppose you're ready to share a little of *your* good fortune with us … ?'

Sir Arthur leaned in close and whispered. 'The, uh, *poop-in-a-can* you mentioned before?'

Grace rolled her eyes. 'Here, take these instead,' she said, picking up her soiled gloves from the top of the pile and handing one each to the boys.

Sir Oliver beamed with pleasure and tucked his glove inside his pyjamas. 'A million thanks! I shall keep it close to my heart.'

Sir Arthur bowed, gave his glove a deep sniff and began to choke. 'I shall – ick! – never wash it – eew! – lest the luck wash off!'

Portia wrinkled her nose. 'Boys are *weird*.'

'I hope the luck lasts until Wondermere

Day,' Sir Arthur said, skipping happily on the spot. 'I shall be crowned champion for sure!'

'No, *I* shall,' said Sir Oliver.

'No, *I* shall,' Grace said. She was daydreaming again. She hadn't meant to say it out loud.

The boys frowned at her. 'You shall *what*?' said Sir Arthur.

'Er,' Grace said, pulling herself together, 'I *shall* be cheering you both on.'

The boys puffed out their chests. Sir Oliver bowed so low Grace wondered if he was going to dive into the moat in his pyjamas. 'And *we* shall endeavour to be worthy of your support.'

A look of deep concern came over Sir Arthur's face. 'But wait! How wilt thou cope without thine gloves? Your delicate hands need protection!'

Grace and Portia shared a smile. 'You're right,' Grace said. 'I feel weak just thinking about it. I think I need a little lie-down – how about you, Portia?'

'Totally,' Portia said.

The girls couldn't hold it in any longer. They burst into giggles and ran off into the castle.

Sir Oliver shook his head. 'Girls are *weird*.'

PRINCESSES DO NOT
SHOP AT THE FOREST MARKET

As the week went on, the princesses grew used to sneaking into the forest. They grew used to riding unicorns and wearing armour too.

Grace had become a very skilled troll-o player indeed. She was a particularly good shot and Poop was turning into a brilliant chaser. Together they scored goal after goal.

Poop's behaviour was improving too,

although all the witch wax in the realm couldn't make his grubby horn gleam. 'I want him to look like a real troll-o steed,' Grace grumbled, clambering into bed. 'I feel like I'm riding a walking dungheap.'

'I've read every book I can find about unicorn care,' Portia said, holding her book open for Grace. 'See? They all say we need giants' toenails.'

'But we don't know any giants,' Grace said, pulling her covers up to her chin.

Portia yawned and blew out the candle. 'You don't get them from giants; you get them from witches. I expect they sell them at the forest market. You could always ask Bram to get you some?'

Grace was glad the room was dark. Her sister wouldn't be able to see that her eyes had lit up and an enormous grin was spreading across her face.

'I *told* you we should've sent Bram,' Portia said, pulling the hood of her cloak further over her face. 'What if someone recognises us?'

Grace held her own hood in place. 'Relax, it'll be fine. Anyway, Bram's doing us enough favours already, fixing up our armour and helping us sneak out to practice. Come on, let's find the witches' stalls.'

The market was the single most fascinating thing Grace had ever seen. There were dozens of little tents and stalls dotted around a wide clearing, all manned by the most fascinating woodsfolk.

An ogre was selling sweet bognuts. 'Picked from my very own bog,' he said, offering Grace a sample. 'Try one!'

'No thank you,' Grace said, moving on quickly past a man selling old sticks.

'Really *nice* sticks.'

They saw a goblin reading fortunes.

'I see a tall, dark, smelly horse …'

And *more* goblins, these ones performing with an imp lady.

Portia applauded. 'OK, I'm glad we didn't send Bram. This is so cool!'

Grace tugged her away. 'We're here for giants' toenails, and we haven't got long. Come on!'

They passed pot stalls, pan stalls, pen and pant stalls, manned by imps, pirates, hobgoblins and – at last – witches.

Portia bought a bag of rare kelpie poo from a particularly knobbly witch with a large purple frog on her shoulder. 'For Bunkum's compost heap,' she explained to Grace. 'A thank-you present for looking after the unicorns when we can't be there.'

Grace picked out a sea serpent's tooth on a string for Bram. 'Thank you,' she said as the witch handed it over, wrapped prettily in parchment and ribbon. 'Do you know where we can find giants' toenails?'

'Behind you,' the witch said, pointing to a towering archway behind the girls.

Grace and Portia walked through it ... but found nothing on the other side. Then the penny dropped. 'Oh, I see!' Grace said, laughing, 'the archway *is* the toenails!'

'But they're enormous,' Portia said, gazing up at the towering nails. 'We'll never be able to carry one of those home.'

'You don't take the whole *thing*,' the witch said, rolling her eyes. Even her frog puffed out its cheeks. 'How much d'you need? I'll clip you a piece off.'

Grace bought the largest clipping she could fit beneath her cloak. 'It weighs a ton,' she grumbled as they made their way back through the woods into the stables.

'Don't complain,' Portia said. She hadn't been able to resist buying a large set of books on enchanted creatures. They bumped against her legs as she walked. 'Carrying this extra weight is all good practice for wearing armour.'

'I guess,' Grace sighed as they crossed the moat and entered the back door to the stables.

Bram was busy mucking out the stalls. 'Did you get everything you needed?'

'And more,' Grace said, handing him his gift. 'We just wanted to say thanks for helping us practise and everything. You're working so hard right now, what with

Wondermere Day coming up.'

'I love it,' Bram said, immediately tying the tooth round his neck. 'But there's no need to thank me. All this is my job, and the rest... well, it's what friends do.'

Grace and Portia pulled off their cloaks, stashed their shopping under a pile of straw and set to work helping Bram muck out the stables.

'Don't wear yourselves out too much,' he said, 'even the knights-in-training aren't working as hard as you two, and they've got the Wondermere Day tournament to prepare for.'

'Blimey,' Portia said, pressing the back of her hand to her forehead. 'Just learning's tiring enough.'

Grace grinned. 'It's fun, though.'

'True,' Portia agreed, letting Leonard eat the final handful of honey grass straight from her hand. 'Have we got time for a quick match now, Bram?'

He grinned. 'I suppose we could squeeze one in.'

Grace put down her rake and sped out of the stable door, shouting, 'Best day EVER!'

DO NOT PRETEND
TO BE A PRINCESS

'You're certainly turning into a fine pair of knights,' Bunkum said, flying through the goal hoop for the eighth time in five minutes. 'Your shape-shifting's improving too, Bram. I can tell you've been practising.'

Bram shook with pleasure. He'd turned himself into a very convincing troll-o goal: a tall post with a large golden hoop at the top.

The hoop moved like a mouth as Bram spoke. 'You really *are* good players. No one would bat an eye if they saw you on the pitch.'

Grace beamed. 'D'you really think so?'

'You'd *definitely* be top scorer,' Portia said. 'I wish my mallet swing was as good as yours. Can we have a time out? I think I just saw a will-o'-the-wisp behind the marshmallow tree ...'

'You're really good too,' Grace said honestly, adding with a smile, 'when you're not getting distracted.' She took a deep breath and cleared her throat. 'Y'know, I've been thinking … I reckon we should enter the tournament on Wondermere Day.'

Portia laughed. 'Very funny.'

'It's not a *bad* idea,' Bram said.

Portia flipped up her visor. 'Seriously?'

'Why not?' Grace shrugged. 'We've put in so much work and we're just as good as the boys.'

'I reckon you're a bit better, actually,' Portia agreed.

Grace grinned. 'If we keep our visors down, no one will know it's us. We're already pretty good and there's still a whole week to go. With a bit more practice, we might even win!'

Portia laughed. 'Imagine that – collecting the trophy from our dad!'

Bram clapped his hands together in

excitement and accidentally turned into a telescope. 'You'll be brilliant. I'll cheer you on all the way.'

'We're really going to do it, aren't we?' Portia said, unable to hide the smile that was spreading across her face.

'You bet,' Grace said.

'I don't want to spoil the moment,' Bunkum said, 'but it's tradition for the princesses to watch the tournament from the royal balcony. You can't *possibly* be in the balcony and down on the pitch at the same time.'

Grace winced. It felt as though an ogre was squeezing its hands around her heart. 'Of course,' she said quietly.

'Oh well,' Portia said sadly, 'it was a lovely thought.'

'Wait,' Grace said, turning to face the two

imps. 'What if *you two* took our places?'

Bram's nose crinkled. 'In the *tournament*?'

'In the *balcony*,' Grace said, eyes sparkling with fresh mischief.

'But we're not royal princesses,' Bram said.

'You *could* be,' Grace said with a smile.

'You mean transform ourselves?' Bram said, looking from Grace to Portia. 'Into *you*?'

'It's forbidden,' Bunkum said seriously – then his face lit up. 'I love it!'

Bram's ears turned pink. 'I could wear a dress!'

'*And* slide down banisters,' Grace said, 'so long as you don't let our dad catch you.'

'His majesty won't notice a thing, imp's honour,' Bram said, turning himself into the mirror image of Grace. Bunkum followed suit, becoming a lookalike of Portia.

'How do we look?' the old imp asked.

'Very pretty,' Grace laughed, 'but you *sound* terrible. You might want to work on your voices before next week.'

Bram pulled the exact face Grace did when she was offended – lips pursed, eyebrows knotted together. 'And *you'll* have to work on your chivalry,' he joked, making his voice higher. 'A true knight would *never* be so rude to a lady.'

It was a wonderfully topsy-turvy afternoon – the imps acting like princesses and the princesses acting like knights. Grace was so happy she could have stayed in the clearing forever. But there wasn't time.

Wondermere Day was fast approaching, and the dragons were growing restless.

DO NOT EAT
ICE CREAM FOR BREAKFAST

At last, Wondermere Day was just a sunrise away.

Tomorrow morning the castle would be packed with spectators from across the realm, ready to enjoy a day's sport in honour of the dragons. But the dragons were all over the place – literally.

One was perched on the clock tower,

cramming grub moss into the mechanism and making the hands run backwards.

Another dragon had clogged more moss into the crank handle of the drawbridge. The bridge was currently stuck half up, half down so no one could cross the moat. The mermaids were doing their best to help the king's men fix it, pulling at the bridge from underneath while the knights pushed from the other side.

As for the state of the turrets ... yuck.

Where gemstones and coins once glittered, grot now festered, giving off a strong pong of dirty socks. The girls' bunting had been hung prettily enough, but it didn't do much to brighten the scene. And if the *castle* looked bad, the dragons looked even *worse*.

Their scales, which normally gleamed like the treasures they collected, were as dull as swamp water. Their tails drooped, their wings sagged and their eyes were cloudy and rimmed with red.

'It really is most troubling,' King Wonder said now, pushing his supper away uneaten. 'What will the crowds think when they arrive in the morning?'

'This is exactly how the Dull Ages started,' Taffy said, sliding his glasses up his furry nose. 'The dragons left and didn't come back for fifty years! Just think – fifty years of bad luck, all because Queen Wonder the Eighth ate ice cream for breakfast. HUGE violation of the rules.'

Grace gazed out of the window at the nearest turret. What a mess. Even she couldn't deny that the dragons were acting strangely.

Portia frowned. 'But how can we be sure it was because of *ice cream*? I mean, maybe the dragons were going to leave anyway? Maybe ice cream had nothing to do with it?'

'Perhaps we should try it in the morning?' Grace suggested. 'An experiment: *to investigate the effect upon dragons of eating ice cream for breakfast.* After all, tomorrow *is* a special occasion.'

Taffy looked horrified. 'Rule number three hundred and forty-one: **DO NOT eat ice cream for breakfast!**'

The king slammed his fist on the table, making everyone jump. 'There'll be *no* experiments, *no* changes and *no* rule breaking. Someone's disturbing the dragons, and when I find out who it is, they're going to be in BIG trouble.'

DO NOT BE LATE
ON WONDERMERE DAY

By breakfast-time, King Wonder was in a much better mood. His servants had worked through the night to smarten up the castle.

'Let's move the banqueting table closer to the windows,' he said to Taffy and the girls. 'We can watch the crowds arriving while we eat.'

Grace was too nervous to eat properly. She

fidgeted with a slice of
toast while she watched
their guests pour through
the castle gates.

They came from all over
the kingdom. Humans and
trolls, fairies and goblins,
elves and pixies, ogres and
witches, imps, banshees
and will-o'-the-wisps …
Everyone was enjoying a
day out as they jostled for
the best seats.

Even the moat was
packed. The mermaids

had made room for visitors
from the Outer Ocean.

The crowds delighted Portia,
but Grace was more interested in
the offerings they brought for the
dragons. She watched now as
they queued to leave their gifts
beneath the castle turrets.

The offerings were
mounting up in huge piles.
There were glittering star
daisies, sacks of sparkle
moss and bags of coins.
All the while, the
king's guard knights

stood their ground, making sure no one came close enough to the turrets to disturb the dragons.

Grace frowned. They were certainly unsettled – flapping and squabbling in their nests. They weren't paying the slightest bit of attention to their gifts, either. Still, she had more urgent things to think about.

Today was the day! She was finally going to become a real knight, playing troll-o in front of the whole realm!

Portia leaned across and whispered in her ear. *'I'm so nervous.'*

'Me too,' Grace said quietly. 'I've only managed four slices of toast.'

'Don't worry,' said Portia, reaching under the table to give her sister's hand a squeeze. 'You'll be brilliant.'

Grace kept hold of Portia's hand while the serving trolls made the room ready for troll-o registration. Taffy Trafalgar stood on his chair, cleared his throat and shouted, 'First knight, please!'

Grace and Portia stood up. It was custom for the royal family to wish each and every knight good luck as they signed up for the tournament. The knights had developed a tradition of shaking Grace's hand in hope that her good luck would rub off on them.

It was a long and boring process which normally drove Grace mad, but this morning she was giddy with excitement. She hurriedly shook each knight's hand in turn as Taffy Trafalgar entered their names on the official troll-o score sheet.

'*Just think*,' Portia whispered, '*you're*

shaking hands with our opponents!'

Grace bit her lip to stop herself grinning. She couldn't wait to get into her armour and play. But there was still one final, vital bit of sneaking to do before the girls could enter the tournament.

They needed to get their names on Taffy's list.

They couldn't possibly register under their *own* names. But they *could* take someone else's spots – just so long as those *someone elses* didn't show up at this afternoon's tournament.

Grace did her best to stifle a yawn.

Sir Oliver and Sir Arthur were right at the back of the line. Typical.

Still, Taffy was working through the knights pretty quickly. Soon the girls could get on with the final part of their plan.

Grace had thought it all through. Bram was ready and waiting in the stables, Bunkum was in position at the tree house. Just as soon as registration was over, everything would be set.

Grace hummed a tune. She scratched her nose. She counted every gargoyle on the vaulted ceiling. (One hundred and twenty-three.) At last, it was Sir Oliver's and Sir Arthur's turn to shake hands with the princesses.

'All done, sire,' said Taffy, tucking the completed registration scroll under his arm.

'Marvellous!' said King Wonder, striding happily off alongside Taffy as they headed out to greet the crowds. 'Better go saddle up, lads, the tournament will be starting at noon on the dot. Come along, girls! The crowd want to greet my beautiful daughters.'

'There in a minute, Dad,' Grace said. Jogging after Sir Oliver and Sir Arthur, she said, 'Hey! Did anyone order some lucky poop?'

The boys stopped in their tracks, clutching one another in excitement. 'Can we *really* have a can?!' said Sir Oliver.

'Better than a can,' Portia said.

Grace bounced her eyebrows up and down. 'Meet us in the stables in one hour, and you can have a whole heap.'

DO NOT SNACK
BETWEEN MEALS

The hour passed so slowly Grace felt as though she were plodding through swamp mud.

The king dragged the girls around the viewing stands to greet the crowds. Grace was sick of curtsying, smiling sweetly and *how-do-you-do*-ing. She was itching to get into her armour. At last, King Wonder agreed that they'd done enough meeting-and-greeting and let them go.

'See you in the royal balcony, dear hearts,' he said cheerily, adding to Taffy as the girls sprinted away, 'Off to find their prettiest dresses, I expect.'

Not likely. The girls headed straight to the stables.

'All set?' Bram asked as they arrived. He was holding the reins of Awesome Sauce, Sir Arthur's unicorn, and Sir Oliver's steed, Legend.

'All set,' Grace said. 'The boys will be here any minute. You'd better hurry!'

Bram led the unicorns out of their stall. 'Come on, Awesome Sauce. Chop-chop, Legend! Time to visit the tree house.'

The girls waved as Bram led the unicorns

into the woods. Grace couldn't help admiring them as they trotted past. The boys' unicorns couldn't be more different from Poop. Muscular, obedient and beautifully fragrant.

The scent of roses still lingered when Sir Oliver and Sir Arthur arrived.

'Can we *really* have a whole heap of lucky poop?' asked Sir Arthur.

'There's no time for that now,' Grace said

urgently. 'You've got more important things to do.'

'We've found out who's been breaking the rules,' Portia said.

'The fiends!' Sir Oliver cried, drawing his sword. 'Where are they? We shall arrest them in the name of Wonder!'

'They're in the forest eating marshmallows,' Grace said.

'They're *what*?' said Sir Oliver.

Sir Arthur

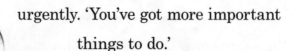

frowned. 'Doesn't *sound* very fiendish.'

'Rule number one hundred and ninety-nine,' Grace said, playing the boys at their own game, '**DO NOT snack between meals**. And, well, there's no easy way to tell you this. The rule breakers are Legend and Awesome Sauce.'

Sir Arthur hung his head in shame. 'The dastardly rascals.'

Grace smiled slyly. 'It's no big deal, the king's bound to forgive them – but it's still against the rules.'

'Absolutely,' Portia said. 'Our father won't care that it

was your unicorns causing the bother, he'll just be delighted with you for fixing everything.'

'What are you waiting for?' Grace said. 'Hop to it!'

Sir Arthur sprinted for the door.

'Wait!' cried Sir Oliver. 'If we leave now, we'll miss the tournament!'

Sir Arthur stopped in his tracks.

Grace shrugged. 'You can't very well play troll-o *here* if your unicorns are out *there*.'

'Good point,' said Sir Arthur. 'Thank you, m'ladies. Thou art truly gracious.'

'No problem,' Grace said, shooing the boys out through the open doorway. 'Take your time, lads.'

The boys bowed hurriedly, knocking heads, then disappeared into the woods. 'Have fun

150

getting stuck into the compost pile!' Grace called as soon as they were out of hearing range.

The girls were still laughing when Bram came back, bringing Bunkum, Poop and Sprinkles with him.

'Sorry it took so long,' Bram said, leading the girls' unicorns to Awesome Sauce and Legend's empty stall. 'Took me a while to persuade the boys' unicorns to wade into the compost heap. They're stuck, but they have enough marshmallows to keep them happy. They won't be going anywhere in a hurry.'

'Those boys won't be either,' Bunkum added. 'Waded right in after them. Really threw themselves into it.'

'I feel kind of bad,' Portia said, burying her fingers in Sprinkles's colourful mane. 'They're missing the tournament because of us. They must have been really looking forward to it.'

'They get to play all the time,' Grace said. 'Anyway, they really are mad about poo, and Dad will be super happy with them when they tell him they found the rule breakers.'

'But they *didn't*, did they?' Portia said quietly. 'It's *us* breaking the rules. Maybe we really *are* bothering the dragons?'

Grace didn't know how to reply, so she pretended not to hear and focused on giving Poop's chin a tickle.

'There's no time to worry about the dragons now,' Bunkum said. 'You need to get your armour on. The tournament's about to begin!'

STABLE BOYS
DO NOT WEAR DRESSES

Sprinkles stood perfectly still while Portia put on his tournament armour, but Poop was not in the mood to cooperate.

Grace had rubbed him all over with a chunk of giant's toenail, dusted powdered toenail in his fur, added a spoonful of the vile stuff into his water trough and even tried brushing his teeth with it. It hadn't made a bit of difference to the way he looked – it had just made him cross.

'No wonder shopping in the forest market's against the rules,' Grace grumbled as Poop deliberately stomped on her foot. 'It's a total rip-off!'

She had an extra hard time convincing Poop to wear a saddle. He'd never worn one before and he wasn't sure he wanted to start today.

'*Don't* stand nice and still while I put this on your back,' she tried.

He *did* stand still – but he *didn't* stop trying to bite her.

'How about I distract him while you sneak round the side?' Bram suggested. 'Ow! He bit me too!'

It took ten minutes and six handfuls of marshmallows, but eventually Poop was saddled, groomed and looking *almost* impressive.

Outside, the royal unicorns were being paraded around the courtyard by their gleaming knights. The crowd's excited chatter drifted into the stables, making Poop even more jittery.

'He might feel better once we're out in the courtyard,' Portia said.

'Maybe,' Grace sighed, pulling on her helmet. 'Well, we're as ready as we'll ever be. It's time you imps got ready too. Have you decided what to wear yet, Bram?'

'I'm thinking something pink and frilly ...' Bram teased.

'Don't you dare!'

He laughed, clapped his hands together and became a mirror image of Grace, only wearing a beautiful sky-blue frock with purple sashes.

'It'll do,' she said, looking him up and down. 'Do I really have that many freckles?'

Bram ignored her and admired his reflection in the back of a shovel. He smoothed his skirts down and flicked his long hair. 'I'm a real princess!'

'And a good one too,' Grace said, 'although

you still sound like an imp.'

'We've been practising, actually,' Bunkum said, transforming himself into Princess Portia and putting on a silly, squeaky voice. 'See? I sound exactly like you!'

'Er, yeah …' Grace said.

Portia's nose crinkled. 'Maybe it would be best if you kept quiet in the balcony.'

Bunkum gave up and spoke in his ordinary voice. 'As you wish. I can't believe we get to watch from the royal box. Best seats in the house! It's so exciting.'

'It's so *nerve-wracking*,' Bram said, wringing his hands together. 'What if I can't hold my shape? I might sneeze and turn into a dustbin.'

'You'll be fine,' Portia said, lacing his bodice tighter. 'Just keep quiet and look pretty – it's what princesses are expected to do, after all.'

Grace grinned. 'They're certainly not expected to take part in the biggest troll-o tournament of the year.'

Bunkum's expression turned serious. 'Are you sure you want to do this?'

'Completely,' Grace said, tugging on her armoured gloves. She picked up her mallet, grabbed Poop's reins and led him to the door. 'I might not be allowed to be a *real* knight, but I can sure play troll-o like one.'

The crowd's roars rattled inside her helmet as she flipped her visor down. 'Come on, Portia, let's show them what we're made of.'

18

GIRLS DO NOT PLAY TROLL-O

'Are you all right, girls?' the king said, briefly turning his attention from the pitch to look at his daughters. 'You don't seem quite yourselves.'

The young princesses *did* look rather uncomfortable. Both were sitting bolt upright, hands tightly balled in their laps. Neither had said a word since stepping on to the royal balcony.

'Not that you don't look lovely,' the king added.

Bram had never had so much hair. He rearranged it to hide his pointy ears, then smoothed his dress over his knees.

The king smiled. 'Very traditional, especially for you, Grace. I thought you might turn up in trousers. Ha!'

Bram was too nervous to respond to the king's joke, but Bunkum attempted an *almost* believable giggle.

The king looked alarmed. 'Are you feeling all right, Portia?'

'I'm fine,' Bunkum squeaked, trying his best not to sound like an imp.

The ball-trolls marched into the courtyard to great applause. The king turned his attention back to the pitch. Taffy Trafalgar, seated behind him, leaped gleefully up and down in his seat.

'COME ON, YOU TROLLS!' he hollered, punching the air.

The king smiled and settled into his throne. His subjects were all around him, his daughters were beside him and his knights were lining up below. This was going be the best Wondermere Day in history. The dragons were going to be utterly delighted.

Grace was utterly delighted.

She was *on the pitch* – playing in the
Wondermere Day Troll-o Tournament in
front of the entire realm. Her sister was
beside her, her friends and father were
watching, and her cheeky wild unicorn was
actually doing as he was told.

Well, doing the *opposite* of what he was
told, actually, but that was just fine.

'*Don't* do what the other unicorns are doing,'
she reminded Poop, keeping her voice low.

Perhaps the giant's toenail was beginning
to take effect – or maybe Portia had been
right and he was just happy to be in the
courtyard. Either way, Poop was in a much
better mood. He gave a snort, bent his front

knees and dipped his horn to the ground in a sort of bow to the king.

Portia was close enough that Grace was able to reach out and give her hand a quick squeeze without anyone noticing. When her sister squeezed back, Grace felt the last of her nerves disappear. Her heart leaped again as Taffy read out the names of the first group of knights to play.

Neither Sir Oliver's nor Sir Arthur's names were called, so Grace and Portia led Poop and Sprinkles to the edge of the pitch with the other knights who weren't playing in the first round.

'SIR FELIX!' Taffy called from the balcony. Down on the pitch, a young knight stepped forward. The ball-troll handed him a blue feather to wear in his helmet. The knight mounted his unicorn and went to join the rest of his team.

'I hope we're on the same team,' Portia whispered to Grace.

'Me too,' Grace said as a second knight was handed a red feather. She stroked Poop's ears while the first two teams were selected. She couldn't wait for the match to begin.

But before it could, a dragon let out a terrible screech from above. The sound startled everyone – especially Sprinkles. He rose up on his hind legs and skittered sideways. Portia panicked, but Grace grabbed Sprinkles by the reins and helped calm him down.

'Don't worry,' Grace said, 'the dragons are probably just excited about the crowds. We're going to be fine.'

And they were. Sprinkles soon settled down as the first match got going. It wasn't the best – both teams were nervous and the players kept missing the goal – but seeing the other knights so jittery reassured Grace. If she and Portia did their best, they'd be just fine. They might even make it as far as the finals.

The screeching dragon had calmed down too. It sat hunched in its nest, back turned on the action, eyes wide as it gazed towards the distant mountains.

Meanwhile, Grace was struggling to keep her eyes on the ball-troll. It had always been easy enough looking down from the royal balcony – you could keep an eye on the whole courtyard from above. But watching at pitch level was a different story.

The unicorns' hooves kicked up dust from the cobbled ground, making it hard to see *anything* clearly. And somehow the ball-trolls looked even faster close up.

They changed direction in a heartbeat, weaving deftly in and out between the unicorns' hammering hooves. They jumped and weaved, turning somersaults in the air as they dodged the knights' swinging mallets.

Team after team of red-and-blue feathered knights faced one another, the highest

goal scorer of each match moving forward into the later rounds. The girls watched twelve whole matches before, at last, Taffy called out Sir Oliver's name.

'That's me,' Grace whispered to Portia, urging Poop towards the centre of the pitch. 'Wish me luck!'

DO NOT ARGUE
WITH THE BALL-TROLL

'Not riding Legend today, Sir Oliver?' the ball-troll asked as Poop ambled lazily across the pitch towards him.

'Legend picked up an injury in training yesterday,' Grace said, hoping the visor would help disguise her voice as well as her face. 'I'm riding his brother.'

The ball-troll raised his hairy eyebrows.

'Funny-looking fellow. What's his name?'

'Um, Valiant?' Grace fibbed.

Poop lifted up his tail and a glittery pile of poo plopped to the cobbles.

'Doesn't suit him,' the ball-troll said, holding his nose. 'Team red,' he said, handing Grace a red feather for her helmet.

Grace led Poop over to the line of red

knights who would be her teammates. She gave Portia a quick thumbs up, indicating a space beside her. There were only two slots left, one on each team. Of course her sister would be playing beside her. Everything was working out perfectly.

Grace turned to face the balcony. She felt a surge of love for her father as she saw him watching earnestly on. *If only he knew!* she thought. Bram and Bunkum both gave her a little wave.

'Round thirteen,' Taffy said, clearing his throat. 'Sir Oliver will be riding against – Aha! His best friend … Sir Arthur!'

'Well, *that's* a bummer,' Grace said, disappointed.

The ball-troll tutted. 'You can't get your own way every day, Sir Oliver. Blue team, Sir

173

Arthur! Chop-chop! Sir Arthur is riding – er, I've no idea.'

'Awesome Sauce is injured too,' Grace told him. 'He's riding Butch!'

'Ladies and gentlemen,' the ball-troll cried, 'please welcome Sir Arthur and his steed for the day, Butch!'

He had to shout it twice more. Portia wasn't used to answering to a different name. Grace yelled, too. 'Wake up, Sir Arthur!'

The crowd burst into laughter as Sprinkles trotted daintily forward. He started to panic again, sidestepping nervously and tossing his pretty mane.

A particularly large ogre pointed and laughed, putting on a baby voice. 'Wook! A sparkly-warkly unicorn! Bless its ickle wickle tootsies!'

That did it. Sprinkles came to an abrupt stop. He stomped his hoof and snorted grumpily.

For a moment, Grace wondered if he might run off towards the stables, but Portia took control. Grace watched proudly as her sister urged him on.

The pair trotted confidently up to Grace and Poop. 'Ready?' Grace said.

'Ready,' said Portia.

Grace grinned behind her visor. 'May the best man win!'

'On the count of three,' the ball-troll said, crouching down, ready to run. 'One …'

The red and blue teams bowed to one another.

'Two …'

They raised their mallets.

'THREE!'

The ball-troll disappeared in a blur of fur and dust. 'Where'd he go?!' said Portia as the other knights gave chase.

'No idea,' Grace said, 'but *I'm* going to find him first!'

Portia laughed. 'No chance! Come on, Butch – giddy-up!'

20

DO NOT DISOBEY
YOUR KING

It was harder than Grace had imagined. Bunkum had been a good ball-troll, but this one was a real athlete. Still, it was even more *fun* than she'd imagined too.

The crowd's cheers spurred them on as they chased one another after the ball-troll. He dashed from one side of the pitch to another, cackling with joy. 'Can't catch me!'

Portia and Sprinkles *almost* whacked
the troll, the crowd gasping as she swung
her mallet in a neat arc, missing it by a
whisker.

'Nice try, mate,' said one of her teammates.

'I'll get him next time,' Portia said.

'Not if *I* get him first,' Grace said, racing
past her. 'Come on, Poop – *don't* catch the
troll!'

Poop hardly needed any coaxing – he was
clearly enjoying his moment in the spotlight.
He might still *smell* disgusting but he was
riding like a dream. It wasn't long before
Grace scored her first goal.

And her second.

And her third.

'Excellent work, Sir Oliver!' said one of her
teammates, slapping her on the back.

Portia soon followed suit. The young witch in charge of the scoreboard could barely keep up.

Six–four, twelve–ten, sixteen all …

By the time the score reached twenty all, the crowd were on their feet. Even the other knights were taking off their helmets, the better to watch the action.

'I knew Sir Arthur was good, but I've never seen him play *this* well,' the king said, applauding as Portia and Sprinkles shot past the balcony.

Taffy agreed, pushing his glasses further up his nose. 'And Sir Oliver has come on in leaps.' He leaned over the balcony to follow the action. 'He's carrying the whole team, sire. If he keeps this up he'll be the highest scorer in history!'

Bunkum and Bram were enjoying the action too. They were so engrossed in the game they'd practically forgotten they were supposed to be princesses. Bram leaped to his feet as Grace scored a phenomenal goal, swinging her mallet backwards and bouncing the ball-troll in off the post.

'GET IN!!' he bellowed.

Everyone turned to look at him – the king, Taffy *and* the surrounding spectators. Bram straightened his tiara, cleared his throat and sat back in his throne, saying in as tinkly a voice as he could manage, 'I mean, *bravo.*'

Not to be outdone, Portia clawed back another goal almost instantly, leaning right out of the saddle to reach the ball-troll. The crowd held their breath, certain the knight would fall …

Not a chance.
Portia's mallet
sliced the air
with a whisper.
She was back in
the saddle just
in time to see
the ball-troll fly neatly through the goal.

By now the cheers had grown deafening.
The score kept growing too.

Thirty all.

Thirty-two–thirty-one.

Thirty-two all.

The other knights on the girls' teams were barely needed. With a minute left on the clock the score was level at thirty-five all. Even the king was on his feet, waiting to see which man would be top scorer in this record-breaking game.

Meanwhile, Grace barely knew the audience was there. She was entirely focused on her next move.

The ball-troll bounced away from her mallet, springing out of reach – at least it *thought* it was out of reach, and for any other knight it might've been.

Grace didn't think twice. In one clean move she was standing on Poop's back, balanced and steady as he sped after the troll.

The crowd went wild. Grace raised her mallet high and swung, sending the ball-troll flying through the goal just as the final bell rang.

The roar was deafening. At last, Grace let herself hear it.

'Don't stand still and take it all in, Poop,' she laughed, leaning right into his ear so he could hear her above the cheers.

It felt as though her heart would burst right out of her armour. She was a real knight – no different to any of the others. Maybe even *better*.

One by one, her teammates dropped to
their knees and removed their helmets in a
mark of respect.

Up in the royal balcony, Taffy was leaping
up and down. 'Remarkable!' he squeaked.
'Nothing like it in all history!'

The king was thrilled. 'Well, that more

than makes up for the sorry state of the dragons.'

He got to his feet, gesturing for the crowds to fall silent. 'Outstanding, boys!' he boomed. 'Highest-scoring match in centuries! You obviously both came here to win. There are lots more matches to play before the champion is crowned. Still, I should like us all to take a moment to acknowledge your achievement.'

Poop and Sprinkles were standing side by side. Grace could hear Portia's armour rattling with nervous excitement.

Bram waved a lace handkerchief at them. 'Well done!'

The king beamed down at them. 'Take your moment in the spotlight, lads. Remove your helmets so the whole realm might know a pair of champions when they see them.'

Portia turned to Grace. 'We *can't!*'

'Spit-spot,' Taffy said. 'Do not disobey your king!'

Grace looked briefly to the exit. She shook her head. 'Dad's right,' she said, 'we've earned this moment. It's time everyone knew what true champions *really* look like.'

Before Portia could stop her, Grace had taken off her helmet.

The crowd gasped. Taffy fainted.

The king turned grey. 'What in the name of Wonder … ?!' he boomed.

Portia removed her helmet too.

'See, Dad?' Grace said. 'I told you. Girls *can* be knights – and it doesn't bother the dragons a bit.'

The king looked utterly baffled. He turned to look at the princesses beside him in the balcony, then looked back to the ones on the pitch. 'If you're down there, who in the realm is *this*?'

Before the imps could explain themselves there was a yell and a commotion at the side of the pitch. One of the guard knights was running into the courtyard, pointing up at the turrets.

'THE DRAGONS!' he yelled. 'THE DRAGONS ARE LEAVING!'

21

DO NOT
BREAK THE RULES

Grace's pride turned instantly to despair.

The guard was right. While everyone had been engrossed in the match, every single nest had emptied.

It was an eerie sight. The dragons were circling slowly above the courtyard. Every time they flew one full circle, another dragon would leave, flapping off towards the mountains, cawing mournfully.

'It's all our fault,' Grace cried.

Portia frowned, then shook her head.
'It's *not* our fault,' she said firmly. 'I've been
thinking, and I'm sure something was
bothering them even *before* we started
breaking the rules. They've been acting
funny for months. I just wish I could put
my finger on why ...'

There was no time to figure it out.

'The dragons are leaving!' the king roared,
waving his arms frantically at his knights.
'Do something, men! As for you two: get to
your room at once! We'll be having serious
words about this later.'

Grace spun Poop around. It was chaos.
The royal unicorns were panicking and the
crowd were in a tizzy too. The king's men

were torn between calming their steeds and calming the crowd. Even the guard knights, no longer having anything to guard, were looking lost.

'We have to help,' Grace said.

'But Dad's so mad at us,' said Portia.

'I know,' Grace said sadly, 'and I feel terrible – about Dad *and* the dragons.' She took a deep breath and tightened her grip on Poop's reins. 'But we're going to put this right. Follow my lead. We're not done breaking rules yet.'

Grace led Poop to the centre of the pitch and ordered him, 'Don't rear up!'

Poop did a brilliant job of disobeying, thrashing his front legs impressively. All the nearby knights turned to watch.

'Everybody, listen up!' Grace yelled. 'If

we're going to fix this, we need every man,
woman, boy and girl to do their bit. Portia: you
work with Bram.'

Grace shouted up to the imps in the balcony.
'Bram – you and Portia round up any nervous
unicorns and take them to the stables!

Bunkum: go unstick Sir Oliver and Sir Arthur from your compost heap. We're going to need all the help we can get.'

Bram and Bunkum both gave her the thumbs up before turning themselves back into imps.

'Excuse me, your majesty,' Bram said, sprinting from the balcony.

'Lovely to meet you, sire,' Bunkum said, giving the king a quick bow before following his son.

The king's mouth was opening and closing like a bogfish's. In his surprise, he staggered, lost his balance and toppled over the edge of the balcony. Taffy shrieked in horror, but Grace didn't hesitate.

She dug her heels into Poop's sides, bringing him neatly beneath the balcony, catching her father before he hit the ground.

The king looked Grace straight in the eyes. He looked so shocked. So disappointed. 'I ought to have known it was you.'

'I'm sorry, Dad,' Grace said. 'I know you're mad, but you'll just have to tell me off later.' She shifted forward to make room in the saddle. 'Take a seat behind me – and hold tight.'

Grace led Poop in a canter past the king's men. 'Pull yourselves together, lads, there's work to do. Reds: you're on crowd-calming duty. Blues: help the guards calm the dragons.'

'Calm the dragons?!' the king cried. '*What* dragons? They've all gone!'

Just then, Portia and Sprinkles came galloping towards them. Portia was riding hands free, gripping Sprinkles with her knees while she had her nose in a book.

'This is no time to read!' the king spluttered. But Grace shushed him.

'What is it?' she asked her sister.

'I don't think the dragons are leaving,' Portia said, thumbing urgently through the pages. 'I've got a theory. But I won't know if it's right until someone gets a look inside a nest.'

Grace didn't hesitate. She was halfway up the nearest turret before the king could stop her.

22

DO NOT CLIMB
THE CASTLE TURRETS

Grace wrapped her hands around the thick tangle of honeysuckle and ivy and began making her way skyward. The king glared after her.

'You're breaking about fifty rules right now,' he yelled.

'I know,' Grace said through gritted teeth, 'and I'll break fifty more if that's what it takes to put things right.'

She had no idea what Portia expected her to find at the top – she only knew she had to climb.

Somehow it felt right to find herself clambering up the turret once again. It was as though even as a toddler she'd known that her destiny waited at the top of the castle turret.

Once or twice she made the mistake of looking down, but she soon got a grip on her fear. Her curiosity was taking over, just like when she'd first arrived at the castle. The answer to the dragons' behaviour would be found in their nests. If her sister was sure, then so was she.

'You'll only make things worse,' the king yelled from below. **'DO NOT disturb the dragons!'**

'Worse?!' Grace hollered back. 'How could things possibly be *worse*?! The dragons are leaving, you're going to ground me *forever*, I've got all my best friends in trouble and nothing will ever be the same again.'

'It'll be even worse if you disturb the nest!' Taffy shouted, coming out of his swoon.

'We have to try seeing things from the

dragons' point of view,' Grace could hear Portia explaining. She imagined her tugging on their father's sleeve and trying to make him see sense. 'Maybe then we'll understand what's really upsetting them.'

'You and your sister are upsetting them,' the king snapped. He added loudly enough for Grace to hear, 'You're upsetting *me*, too.'

'I'm sorry, Dad,' Grace called down, 'truly I am! But I have to see this through.'

Grace was almost at the top. Hand over hand she climbed, her heart in her mouth. Climbing had been easy enough when she was a little girl, curious and fearless. It was *not* so easy for a full-grown princess in armour – especially when she was feeling so bad.

Luckiest girl in the kingdom? Not a

chance. Her father would never forgive her. Being a knight meant nothing if he was disappointed in her.

But maybe she could still put things right. Just a little higher …

Grace pulled herself over the top of the turret and rolled into the nest. It looked very different to her first visit. There was grub moss everywhere. Scratchy, non-glittery, filthy grub moss. Even so, it felt oddly familiar, like coming home. The smoky, cosy smell, the scratchy twigs …

The weird *snuffling noise*, though? That was new. And if the dragons had *left*, what was that, moving under her feet?

'What can you see?' the king called up after her.

'**AN EGG!**' Grace yelled. '**TWO EGGS!**

23

RULES WERE
MADE TO BE BROKEN!

The dragons came back later that night,
greeted by applause from the delighted crowd.

They brought more grub moss to warm
any eggs that hadn't yet hatched. Grace took
the spyglass Portia offered her.

'See?' Portia explained. 'The grub moss is
softer than coins and gems. It's gentler on the
babies' scales.'

'Amazing,' Grace said, wishing she were back in the nest so she could hug them.

'I should've known they were nesting,' Portia said. 'I've read so much about how other magical creatures behave when babies are on the way. It seems so obvious now.'

'The good luck of the realm is guaranteed,' the king said, hugging the girls tightly. 'For the first time in history, Wondermere will have a new generation of dragons!'

Not wanting to give up the spyglass, Grace asked Bram to turn himself into a telescope so everyone could take a turn at seeing just how cute the baby dragons were.

'They really are adorable,' Taffy said, wiping a happy tear from his cheek.

'And *stinky*,' said Bunkum. An adult dragon was teaching the baby to poop over

the edge of the turret. Delighted, Bunkum pocketed the mess, saying, 'I'll add it to my heap.'

'And a magnificent heap it is too,' said Sir Oliver.

Sir Arthur stood beside him, covered in poo and beaming up at the nest. 'It was an honour to spend the morning knee-deep in your magnificent collection.'

'We are blessed indeed,' Sir Oliver agreed.

'You're welcome, any time,' Bunkum said proudly, shaking their filthy hands.

Portia scribbled a note in the margin of one of her books. 'Someone needs to write a new book,' she said, drawing a line through a whole page. 'The dragons have never laid eggs before. It's all so new!'

Taffy Trafalgar straightened his spectacles and cleared his throat. 'I'd be delighted to rewrite the history books, if his majesty allows … ?'

The king smiled broadly. 'I can't think of a better man for the job.'

Taffy clicked his heels together, saluted and dashed off to grab ink and a quill.

'I can think of a better *girl*,' Grace said quietly to Portia. '*You'd* do a brilliant job, if only they let girls write books.'

The king raised a bushy eyebrow. 'Is that so?'

Grace blushed. 'You weren't supposed to hear that.'

The king smiled. 'Perhaps I needed to. But on this particular occasion, we'll leave the writing to Taffy – my *girls* have something even more important to do.'

Grace undid the clasps on her armour and began to take it off. 'Let me guess,' she said. 'Come on, Portia. Let's go to our room and think about what we've done.'

'Wait a minute,' the king said, stroking his beard thoughtfully. 'Let's just list all the rules you've broken, shall we?'

He counted on his fingers. 'You stole armour, you stayed up all night, you took

troll spit without asking, you sneaked out of
the castle, you tamed wild unicorns, you
visited the illegal forest market, you led two
of my knights into the woods and almost
drowned them in dung—'

'For which we are eternally grateful,' said
Sir Arthur.

'—you lied to me
repeatedly AND you
entered the troll-o
tournament,
even though it's
*strictly against
the rules* for
girls to
play—'

'She scored
some wicked

goals, though,' Bram said, putting an arm around her.

'Sorry, Dad,' Portia said.

'Me too,' Grace said, looking her father in the eye. 'We didn't *want* to lie.'

The king smiled sadly. 'And you wouldn't have *needed to* if it weren't for the rules. You've been right all along. A little change here and there won't hurt the dragons. In fact, it'll do us *all* the power of good.'

He pulled Grace and Portia in for a hug. 'Well done, my best girls – my bravest, most brilliant *knights*.'

He raised his voice now so the whole crowd could hear.

'All hail Sir Portia, my new champion of dragon studies!'

Portia squealed with delight, high-fiving

Grace, the imps and the poo-stained knights.

'And all hail Sir Grace,' the king said.

Grace held her breath. What on earth could she possibly *champion*? Mischief? Toast eating? Disobedient unicorns?

'... Champion of Wondermere's brand new *mixed* troll-o league!'

'Boys *and* girls?' Grace gasped. 'Playing *together*?'

'Naturally,' the king said with a shrug. 'Why in all Wonder *wouldn't* they?'

The women and girls in the audience cheered so loudly Grace felt her heart might burst with joy. She really *was* the luckiest girl in the kingdom.

She threw one arm around her sister and the other in the air, shouting, **'LET'S GO BREAK SOME RULES!'**

LOOK OUT FOR GRACE'S NEXT EPIC
ADVENTURE!
COMING SOON!

Wondermere is expecting a VERY IMPORTANT visitor:
the mermaid queen of the Outer Ocean. That means
FRILLY DRESSES and BEST BEHAVIOUR — and absolutely
NO RULE BREAKING.

But when Grace rescues a DRAGON'S EGG from the
Wondermere Castle moat, suddenly she finds herself
babysitting a BIG SECRET.

One teeny tiny dragon couldn't POSSIBLY disturb
the royal visit ... could he?